MW01168704

mary anne mohanraj

perennial

a garden romance

For Arthur, who taught me how to garden,
not knowing how much I'd need to...

....and for Drs. Robinson, Perez, and Small,
their staffs, and the nurses in the Loyola Hospital
chemo ward; thank you again for your excellent and
compassionate care. Every little kindness was felt.

Author's Note

In February of 2016, I was diagnosed with breast cancer. Over the course of the following year, I was treated with five months of chemotherapy, lumpectomy surgery, and six weeks of radiation. I am now, knock on wood, cancer-free.

This little book intercuts poems I wrote over the course of that year with a gardening story. I'm an enthusiastic amateur gardener, and over and over during treatment, I took great solace in my garden and the philosophy it offers.
I hope this book offers you solace and joy as well.

Mary Anne Mohanraj
December 2017

One

"CAN I HELP you?" The woman in the front section of Devan McLeod's garden shop had been wandering aimlessly about the store for a full twenty minutes. Usually he tried not to pester the customers; after eleven years in America, he still hadn't dropped all of his more reserved habits. His Scottish father had been the strong, silent type, but his Indian mother came from shopkeeper roots, and he could just hear her scolding him now. *Take care of your customers, son, and they'll take care of you.* He really ought to Skype them; it'd been too long.

"I'm sorry," she said, blinking up at him. January in Oak Park meant that she had entered his shop swathed in what his wife had called sleeping bag coats—the kind of puffy coat that covered you from head to ankles. But Devan kept the shop warm and humid, for the customers as well as the plants, and the woman had already unbuttoned her coat, stuffed gloves in her pocket, and unwrapped her scarf, revealing brown curls, bright blue eyes, and a mouth that looked like it wanted to smile. "I don't really know what I want—your window just looked so lovely."

"I try," Devan said, smiling. January meant paperwhites and amaryllises, and his shop window featured a splendid array of white blooms on tall green stalks, supported by graceful copper stakes. It had come out nicely, if he did say so himself. Manju had done all the displays, back in the day, but after five years without her, he'd developed his own style—a little more restrained, less exuberant than what she would have done. So far, the customers seemed to like it; the store was still paying its bills, at a time when many others had gone under. Most small businesses survived on the tiniest of profit margins.

His mother would have said it was the tea and hospitality that kept people coming. Which reminded him, "Do you want some tea? And there's some shortbread on the tray."

"Oh, that would be so good—" the woman walked across the store to the little table where an array of teas waited, and an electric kettle. She poured herself a mug, not bothering with sweetener or milk, and cupped it in hands that trembled a little. She drank the tea straight off, though it must have been scaldingly hot, and Devan winced for her. Then she stood there, staring at a table displaying succulents, for an unconscionably long time. Long enough that Devan *had* to ask, "Are you all right, miss?" She wasn't a miss, exactly, but not a ma'am either—about his own age, he'd guess, early thirties.

"I'm sorry," she said, turning to face him. The mug was still in her hand, and she looked at it, startled. "Where should I—"

Devan came forward to take it from her, and their hands touched, brown to white, and despite the humidifiers he had running, the air was still dry enough to make a spark. Invisible, but felt. She smiled up at him, apologetically. "I'm sorry. I got some strange news today."

"Bad news?"

"I don't know yet. Maybe."

"Here, hold on a sec." Devan wasn't sure why he was doing this—just because she looked lost, and he wanted to see what her face would look like if it were smiling, as it was meant to. He ducked into the back room, where the last of the Christmas décor lingered, and clipped off a sprig of holly. A few twists of floral tape, a pin, and now he had a little holly pin. He brought it back into the main room, and handed it to the woman, who looked bemused.

"Holly—it's still green in the darkest part of the year; it's a traditional symbol of hope, protection, and victory."

She smiled then, and carefully pinned it to her scarf. "That's exactly what I need—thank you. What do I owe you, for this and the tea?" Her smile was exactly what he'd thought it would be—brightening a sweet face to startling beauty. Devan couldn't help smiling in response.

"Please, the holly is on the house. And the tea is always complimentary. Come back when you want a plant to brighten your home."

The woman nodded. "I'll do that, though I'm afraid I tend to kill plants, and if you could see the disaster that is my home right now...well."

"Some of our plants are remarkably hardy," Devan said solemnly. "They resist the most determined plant murderers."

She laughed—and if he'd thought her smile was sweet, her laugh was ten times better. "Good to know," she said.

"I'm Devan, Devan McLeod."

"Katherine Smith. Kate."

"Nice to meet you, Kate. Come back soon."

"I will," she said. She looked better now, less lost. As she buttoned her coat and disappeared into her scarf, Devan held onto her words like a promise. Oh, Kate probably didn't mean them—he knew that. It was the sort of thing you said to shopkeepers to be polite. But Oak Park was a small town; once you met someone, you were always running into them again when you didn't expect it. One way or another, he hoped he'd be seeing Kate again soon.

When You Have Breast Cancer

Friends rush in for overdue
mammograms, even the ones who were
resisting going at all,
afraid of what they'd find.

Husbands are kinder to their wives,
hold them tight at night,
seeing a future without them.

It can make you cranky;
this should be about you,
but now it's also about them.

You let it go.

May something good come of this—
more check-ups and kisses.
We should all be kinder to each other,
to ourselves.

Two

KATE DROVE OUT of the hospital parking lot, stomach churning. The biopsy results were back, confirming breast cancer. The overall prognosis was very good; she'd almost certainly be fine. Still, it meant she faced a year of treatment in whichever hospital she decided to go with. Chemo, surgery, radiation, most probably. A long year, and it meant she had to make a choice.

She could stay here, in this little village where she had just started to put down roots, or she could flee back to New York, with its top hospitals, top doctors, and all her old friends. She had come to Oak Park with such hopes. Her mother would be pushing her to come back.

Kate had only been here a month—she hardly knew anyone. Which might explain why she parked in one of the village downtown lots, climbed out of the car, and walked straight into Devan's shop. She hadn't seen the man in weeks, had barely exchanged a dozen sentences with him—but he'd been kind, that terrible day, when the first suspicious mammogram results had come in. She'd been almost positive that it would turn out to be nothing. Almost.

When Kate opened the door, red hit her, a wave of color, delighting her eyes. Red roses mostly, offered in single stems, big bundles, mixed bouquets. Of course—tomorrow was Valentine's Day. She had forgotten, but the red was a welcome change from pink. Every brochure the hospital gave her seemed to have pink ribbons decorating it, and the nurses in women's health all wore pink scrubs, head to toe. Walking in there was a little like stepping into a plush pink womb—comforting, in its own way, but overwhelming. This was better.

"Kate Smith. Black tea, straight up." The proprietor smiled at her, and tiny lines formed at the corners of his eyes. She felt the familiar urge in her fingers, the longing for a pencil, so she could sketch him. Oddly adorable— those lines made him look younger, instead of older. She was guessing he was in his late thirties or early forties, several years older than herself.

"You remembered my name. *And* how I take my tea." Devan was already pouring her a mug, handing it to her. His hands were broad, brown-skinned, callused. They looked strong.

"How could I forget such a bonnie wee lass?" He laid on the Scottish accent thickly for that one, and she couldn't help laughing. It felt good; Kate couldn't remember the last time she'd laughed. A month ago, probably. She cupped her hands around the mug and took a long draught. It was good, though she shook her head no when he offered the plate of biscuits. Kate could tell by looking that they were dry and lacking in butter. Her life was difficult enough right now without adding bad cookies to the mix.

"I'm not so wee as all that. Although I suppose next to you..." Devan was a tall drink of water, as her father would have put it, a solid foot taller than she was. Kate wished she could talk to her dad now—she wanted that so badly it hurt. He would've told her what to do—he wouldn't need to tell her, actually, because if he were still alive, living in New York, she would never have left. He had always been able to deal with her mother, somehow, and mom hadn't been so bad, when he was still around. Maybe it was the grief that had made her so controlling—that was the kind explanation. When Kate had finally left New York, it had felt like coming up for air, after too long underwater. There was only so long you could hold your breath.

"So what can I do for you today? A rose for your sweetheart? Or better yet, a dozen? Two? A shopkeeper needs to eat, and the taxes in this town are ruinous for an honest man." Devan sounded like he meant it.

"I don't have a sweetheart." And that hurt a little too, although it hardly mattered in the midst of missing her dad and cancer. Jake had said he loved her, but he loved New York more, as it turned out. She drank a little more tea.

"Then the men of this land are fools," Devan said, very seriously.

Kate said, "You say that like you've only just arrived." She was surprised; the shop seemed established.

Devan shrugged. "Oh, it's been a little more than a decade; I came to the States right after college. But it's not so easy as you'd think, to move to a strange place and adapt yourself to their ways. Something is always lost, left behind."

Was there really anything she still wanted in New York? She had had a good life, a predictable, safe life. Kate had had friends and family there, who had approved of her work as an accountant, the stability that career offered. But maybe that just the shell of her old life, now outgrown. Perhaps she was better off doing this alone. "Maybe you're better off without it."

"Maybe," he agreed. They were both quiet for a moment, until Kate finally shook herself out of her silence. She put the mug down on the counter.

"I really don't want roses, but maybe something else? Do you even have anything else?" She turned around, taking in the rest of the front room. Roses, roses, as far as the eye could see. Beautiful, and heavy with scent; she'd thought that modern roses weren't supposed to be strong-scented? Maybe Devan had special varieties; he didn't seem the sort to use fake scent to entice customers.

He said crisply, "Anyone running a garden store who doesn't provide an abundance of roses the day before Valentine's Day is a complete and utter fool who deserves to lose his shop to the taxman. And the taxes in this town are enough to ruin a man. You happened to come in during a quiet moment, but just wait—we'll soon be slammed with desperate boyfriends and husbands who put things off 'til the last minute." Devan smiled. "But I'll admit, roses are a bit predictable, at least right now. There are plenty of other flowers in the back rooms—how do you feel about amaryllises?"

"I don't really have an opinion." Those were tall, red flowers, weren't they? The grocery store sold them at Christmas, along with the poinsettias. "Honestly, I don't know much about flowers." Kate had never had time to learn—had kept her head down studying, then working, working, working, too often in windowless rooms, staring at rows of numbers. She had liked numbers, once upon a time.

"February is the best time for amaryllises, I think. Some shops would already be offering daffodils and such, but I like to save those for April. Every flower in its proper time—follow me." Devan led her through an open doorway, through a short hallway, and into a second large room. This one was more of a working space, with a large trough sink and a broad metal work table. But one wall was solid windows, and against them were rows of green glass shelves which, at the moment, held an array of amaryllises. Classic red, but also pink and white; striped, edged, and ruffled, small and medium and huge. Kate had had no idea they came in such variety.

He reached down a white bloom, edged in a thin line of red. "This one is Picotee—it suits you. It's small and delicate, but still strong."

Kate was afraid she was blushing. "It's lovely."

Devan handed the flower to her; he was standing almost too close. Almost, but not quite. He smelled good, like pine trees and woodsmoke. "There's a story that goes with them. Amaryllis was a timid nymph, who fell in love with a shepherd—but the fool didn't love her back."

"Tragic," she said, smiling.

Devan nodded. "Indeed. So she followed an oracle's advice; she dressed in white and appeared at his door for thirty nights. Each night, she pierced her heart with a golden arrow. When the shepherd finally opened his door, there before him had grown a striking crimson flower, sprung from the blood of Amaryllis's heart. So the flower has come to mean pride, determination, and radiant beauty."

Kate swallowed; her mouth was suddenly dry, and she wished she still had her tea. "That's a sad story."

Devan shrugged. "Many of the best ones are, I'm afraid."

"I have cancer." Kate hadn't meant to say it—she hadn't told anyone yet, and here she was telling someone who was still basically a complete stranger. Maybe that's what made it possible.

Devan's eyes darkened. "I'm sorry, lass."

She shook her head. "Don't worry. I'm probably going to be fine."

"Well. That's good," he said, cautiously.

"It's going to be a fight. But I can handle it." At least for the moment, Kate felt like she actually could. She could borrow some determination from the amaryllis. "I'll take this. And I'll be back in April for the daffodils."

"That sounds like an excellent plan." Devan hesitated a moment, as if he wanted to say something more. But in the end, he just said, "Let me wrap that for you. It's too cold for her to go outside all bare; she needs a little protection."

Kate followed him back to the counter. She wouldn't mind a little protection herself. Well, that's what the oncologists were for, and the chemo and the radiation and whatever else they threw at this thing. Somehow, between one room and the other, she'd decided—she was staying in Oak Park. She was going to chase her dreams, in whatever time the cancer treatments allowed her. And that decision didn't have anything to do with Devan; she had no time for romance right now. A spark leapt between their fingers when he passed her the wrapped pot, but that was just February, dry air, and static electricity.

Still, she felt better, having told someone.

Now, she just had to tell her mother.

SANGUINE, MOSTLY

You seem so calm.
My doctor says this to me, when I call her
two days after diagnosis, ready
with lists of oncologists to consider,
my calendar open. Let's get this thing done.

She sounds almost worried that I
do not sound more worried, that perhaps
the truth hasn't sunk in. I rush
to reassure her that I have my weepy
moments. I'm just action-oriented;
I like to make plans and follow through.
I am more ready than she is.

The waiting is the hardest,
more than one person has said.
I doubt that's true, but it's certainly
maddening. I may procrastinate
unpleasant e-mail, tedious grading,
but when the truly terrible looms,
I'd rather dive in, headfirst.

The Greeks divided us by humour:
the excitable were choleric and melancholic;
the calm, phlegmatic and sanguine.
I am steadiest in the morning, when
I can do research with a clear head,
take calls, make plans. I am even
calm enough to reassure the people
who love me, many of whom possess
a more mercurial temperament.

I'm glad to do that for them, to
make small jokes, laugh it off.
Then evening arrives, and the weight
of the day descends, with all its petty
frustrations and greater fears.
I take to my bed, curl around
the drowsy dog, pull the covers high.

You may just sail through this,
my doctor says. Maybe. Maybe not.

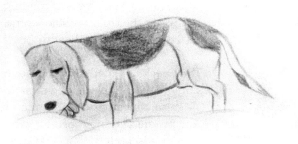

Three

THE SHOP'S PHONE rang, and Devan almost dropped the clay pot in his hand. He'd been distracted, worried by a patch of mold that had appeared on some of the bulbs he was forcing—too much moisture in the fridge, probably. But it was late in the season to be repotting spring bulbs. He really shouldn't be doing this, he should be bent over the computer, staring at the accounts, seeing if there was any way to squeeze a little more profit out before the tax bill came due—Ring! Ring! Right. One thing at a time.

Devan put the clay pot down and lifted the phone from its cradle—a landline still felt more reliable for the shop than relying on his cell alone, though his friends mocked him for it. Hello, you've reached The Rose & Thistle—how can I help you? It was the name of his da's favorite pub, back home, but it had seemed like a good name for a flower shop here.

"Devan?"

"Yes?" The voice was familiar, but he couldn't quite place it.

"It's Kate, Kate Smith."

The lovely brown-haired girl. Devan's voice warmed, almost against his will. "It's good to hear from ye, lass. What can I do for you? It's not quite daffodil time yet."

She laughed, but the laugh sounded forced. "You remembered. I know it's only March. But I could really use a little floral cheer right now."

Devan wouldn't have asked, not wanting to pry into her affairs—she probably got too much of that from well-meaning folks. But she was the one who had raised the subject... "Are the treatments going poorly, then?"

"Hah! If only." The frustration was keen in Kate's voice. "They haven't even started yet—I thought they'd rush me in right away, but instead there's round after round of tests. Biopsies, MRIs....it's been weeks and weeks now. They keep telling me soon..."

Devan tried to make his tone cheery. "Well, I'd try to take it as a good sign. If they thought you were a really sad case, then they wouldn't mess around with a lot of tests."

"I suppose you're right." She was quiet a moment, and then added, "I guess in your line of work, you end up dealing with a lot of sick people."

Aye, and plenty of death too, though he wouldn't say that to her now. Flowers couldn't cure much—couldn't really cure anything, not even an angry heart, as too many men bearing his roses in hopeful apology had learned to their sorrow. Devan did try to warn them that the roses alone likely wouldn't be enough. Still, sometimes flowers softened the worst of times. "A few," he only said, mildly. "So you should trust me on this."

She sighed. "I will then. I'm sorry I'm not coming into the shop, but these tests have eaten up so many hours, I'm basically chained to this house right now. I thought you might be able to send something over. If your shop does deliveries?"

"We have a boy who runs things around for us, no worries." Devan was tempted to run it over himself, but that wasn't what she'd asked for, was it? Kate might think he meant something more by it than a friendly gesture. Best not spook her—she had enough to be worrying about right now. "Now, what are you thinking of? It's a bit early to be planting outdoors—the ground's not really soft enough to work."

"Oh, no." Kate actually laughed at that, sounding startled. "I mean—it would be lovely to have a garden here someday, but I couldn't possibly start one now. First I have to get this house in order; you wouldn't believe what a disaster it is."

"Every house, no matter how messy, deserves at least a wee garden. But there's time, no doubt." Devan was readying a host of early spring bulbs, the ephemera that were here one week and gone the next. Those were lovely: scilla and muscari, checkered fritillaries and chionodoxa, and after those, the crocuses—oh, but wait. The girl was impatient, eager for the treatment to start. Start sooner, to be done sooner; he could understand that urge. "You need snowdrops."

"Oh?"

"Best to plant the bulbs in your yard in the autumn—they're just starting to peek up now, pushing their way through the snow." He hadn't forced any this year, but there were some growing in the backyard, in between the stepping stones; he could dig them and pot them up for her. He had a mix of types—Hippolyta, Viridapice, Ophelia; he could give her a good variety. "Snowdrops come along with the first perennials, the hellebores—when those two show up, you know spring is right around the corner. I'd like to plant a thousand snowdrops somewhere, or maybe two thousand, or three—a little sea of snowdrops, like white foam on the waves."

He coughed, a bit embarrassed at himself; his da liked to go on like that, poetical. Devan used to gently mock his father for it, but apparently, he'd picked up some of the habit. Maybe it ran in the blood.

"Sounds nice." Devan could hear the smile in Kate's voice. "My yard is a sea of mud and slush right now. I blame the dogs."

"You have dogs? I knew you were the right sort." He

hadn't gotten another since auld Max had gone, hadn't had the heart. But it cheered him, to think of her with a few dogs gamboling about.

"Shelter mutts, two of them. Mostly beagle, I think. I don't know what I'd do without them." Emotion evident in her voice, gone a little shaky.

"Well, I'm glad you have them to cheer you." He wanted to keep her on the phone, but best to let her go, let her regain her composure. "I'll have Adam bring over the snowdrops this evening, if that's all right. He has school, and then play rehearsal after. Would around seven work?"

"That'd be perfect. I'm at the corner of Clinton and Jackson, the grey Victorian. Just have him ring the bell."

"Ah, you're just around the corner." Devan's breath seemed to come a little faster; he sternly told it to calm down. She was eight blocks away; he knew that house, had walked past it enough times. It didn't seem right for her—it had always looked so sad, almost desolate. And the yard was a disaster; Devan was surprised the Village hadn't fined her for failing to keep it up properly. He could take care of that for her....what nonsense!

He shook his head, clearing away the thought. It was because Kate was sick, that was all. But that didn't mean she needed him charging up, like a knight come to rescue some damsel in distress. If she actually needed his help, she'd ask. "Well, we'll have that to you this evening." He took her payment details, and then said goodbye, laying the phone back on its cradle.

There was really no reason to feel so happy, but Devan couldn't seem to help himself; he found himself whistling, as headed out back to dig up all of his snowdrops. *By yon bonnie banks, and by yon bonnie braes, where the sun shines high on Loch Lomond. Where me and my sweetheart were ever wont to be, by the bonnie bonnie banks of Loch Lomond...*

HAMMOCKS OR,
THE REST DEFINES THE MEASURE

Descending to a dream, the heat
of Orlando rises from the tarmac,
thick and moist, almost enough to drown
the beat of the word that punctuates
each hour, the syncopation to
the last six weeks, the word her friends
find hard to say—and she does too;
they talk around it instead. Diagnosis
is better. Have you heard about my—
and a relief when they have, no need to lay
it out again. The odds are good, but still,
but still. The clink of glass against ice
against glass against tables, the dull roar
of a convention's worth of conversations,
packed into too small a space; she grows
hoarse trying not to say it all again, trying
mostly to talk about anything else. They
follow her lead. The young ones shocked
though she's old to them, silver-threaded,
in the field longer than they can remember,
since before some of them were born. Age-mates
are quick to offer ardent reassurance, ask
for details, immerse themselves in this
disaster that may come to them too, sooner
than expected. The older generation are quiet;
know better than to make any promises.
We're all pulling for you, is the most
they'll say; they've lost too many friends
to offer more. It's all a comfort, in its way;
there is no right, no perfect thing to say;

let's have another drink as good as anything,
or how's the new book coming? She immerses
herself in words until she's stuffed to the brim,
smothering the rigid beat below,
then retreats to swim long, clumsy laps
feeling muscles move the way they're built for,
(soon, there'll be no swimming, doctors say)
under a perfect sun which cares nothing for her.
Tired at last, all the voices muted,
she takes to the hammock and stares up,
swallowing the sky above the palms,
noon-bright, then dusky-dark. The lake,
built by human hands, houses fluting birds,
aggressive raccoons, a sleepy alligator that
thankfully does not dare the bank, a loud
cacophony of nature, sights and sounds
and even smells, rank and lush and living,
always living. The last hour, wine in hand,
she leans on the wood railing, worn smooth;
how many have come to lay down care,
or try to? Trochee, the beat, the word beneath
it all. Dragonfly wings catch the light;
a green lizard pauses, puffs out its throat,
red polka dots against a white field,
bright as measles, as sunlight, as love.

Four

SHE HADN'T PLANNED to come as far as his store; Ginger and Cinnamon had been restless, wanted a longer walk than usual, with the scent of spring in the air. So instead of just going around the block, Kate had taken them for a long ramble, enjoying the warmth that encouraged her to stretch her legs, let her unzip her jacket. Her fingers brushed the bandages on her chest; they'd inserted the port beneath her skin two weeks ago, a little mechanism that would take the chemo medicine and run it directly through a tube to the vein in her neck.

Kate kept catching herself running her fingers along the tube, palpable beneath the skin, though not so visible. A casual glance wouldn't reveal that she was now a cyborg: part human, part machine. The doctors had promised the port would make this easier, so that each chemo infusion was an easy quick prick, rather than a search for veins in the arm or hand that might degrade and collapse over time. It all made sense, she supposed, but it was still a bit unnerving.

Better to just walk, let the rush of blood push the worries out of her mind, let the dogs tug her where they wanted to go. Past the little tea shop and the antique store, the host of restaurants and the new place that rented bikes. Maybe she should buy a bicycle–the doctor had said she should exercise as much as she felt up to, over the next several months, that she should live her life as fully as she could. It made sense, but sometimes it was all too much to consider.

The biggest problem was still the house. Kate's mind returned to it, over and over, like a tongue poking at a sore tooth. It had seemed such a windfall, when the great-uncle she'd never known had died and left her his old house. Her mother had wanted her to sell it, of course—it would've been the smart thing to do. But it was in terrible condition; he'd gotten quite old and frail at the end, it seemed, hadn't done anything to keep the place maintained.

Kate had flown out to see it, meaning to hire someone to fix it up enough to sell. But when she'd climbed out of the taxi and seen the place, she'd fallen in love. Not so much with the house itself, though it had beautiful bones under the peeling grey paint. A wide front porch that wrapped around, a square turret, tall windows, and chimneys that hinted at fireplaces within. That was all promising, but it was the street that captured her, the long avenue of trees casting shade, the smiles from the neighbors passing by. It was so much quieter than New York. And then there was the basement, with plenty of space for all her supplies, room for a long table to work at, and even enough half-height windows to let in a good amount of natural light. It was as if the house was whispering to her—*Here, you can finally do your real work.*

"Coming in? The daffodils are here."

Kate was startled out of her reverie—she had apparently stopped walking in front of his shop, standing there for long enough that Devan had come and opened the door. He grinned at her, and for a moment, her heart tumbled in her chest. A little flip of excitement that she sternly stuffed down. Devan didn't think of her that way; she was just a customer, probably more troublesome than most. And she had no time for romance now, in any case. Three priorities—

clean up and fix the house, launch her business, treat the cancer. That was enough to keep two women busy, or three. There was no room for a love life as well.

But it surely wouldn't hurt to smile back, so she did, and his smile grew wider. Oh, careful, Kate. "I can't come in–I have my boys." She gestured down at the pair of them, who were now inquisitively sniffing at his pants legs, poking their noses past him, into the intriguing scents of the shop. "Cinnamon and Ginger, meet Devan."

"Pleased to meet you, lads." He bent down to pet them, and Cinnamon burst into an ecstasy of barking. Ginger, as usual, was silently appreciative, leaning into the scratch. "I'd invite them in, but I'm actually in the midst of doing the April displays, so it's a bit chaotic in here, and I fear they would not help matters."

She could see past him, where boxes sat open on the floor, with ceramic rabbits and nests of blown glass eggs peeking out of newspaper wrapping. Kate let out an involuntary sigh.

"Something wrong?" He asked it lightly enough, and she was grateful for it. Devan knew about the cancer, but unlike some of her friends in New York, he seemed to understand that there were other things to think about in life, that there could, in fact, be things wrong that didn't have anything to do with her health. Kate felt bad about it, but she had mostly stopped talking to her New York friends over the past few months; it was too difficult. It was easier to be silent. After all, she had the dogs for company.

Still, he deserved an answer. "It's just a little too reminiscent of my house. I inherited it from a relative who passed, and I've spent three solid months packing up and selling his things." Kate had had to keep working, of course, but freelance accounting work could be done from home, in between packing up boxes; that was the good thing about her job. And the numbers were soothing, even if they didn't exactly offer a creative outlet. "If I never see another cardboard box again..."

"Do ye need a hand?"

Her heart did that little flip again. "Oh, no. I couldn't. That's so kind of you to ask. Besides, I'm almost done." Not quite true—she'd finished packing up the first floor, but there was still plenty to do in the warren of little rooms upstairs. What Kate was really itching to get to was the basement, but that would be her reward, when she'd finished the rest... "It's really very kind of you." Kate was repeating herself, but she couldn't help it. Devan's warm eyes on her made her nervous, made her feel like a teenager again. "I should get going."

"Wait!" He ducked back in, letting the door swing closed behind him, so she waited, tightening the leashes so the dogs wouldn't try to tug her into the shop after him. Sometimes they thought they could walk through glass.

"Here—" He was back, and handing her a little plastic green pot, stuffed full of bright yellow daffodils. She didn't know much about flowers, but these, even she recognized. Her hospital had a big campaign going: Daffodil Days, to raise funds for cancer support. Photos of the flowers were everywhere, but they couldn't really capture the fresh delight of these blooms.

"Daffydowndillies," Devan said, smiling. "That's what my da always called them; it's an old name. You just pop that into a nice cachepot and you're good to go. Sprinkle a little water in there every few days—they should last for weeks."

"They're lovely." Kate fumbled, trying to reach her wallet with the hand that was holding the leashes; the other was fully occupied with the pot of flowers.

"Oh, dinnae fash yerself, lass. It's on the house."

She smiled, but with a bit of concern. "You can't really keep a business going if you keep giving away your stock, you know."

He chuckled. "Yes, that's what Manju always said. She said I'd run it into the ground without her."

"Manju?"

"My wife. Ex-wife," Devan hurried to add. "We opened the shop together."

"I'm sorry." So he'd been married. She wondered how recently.

"I'm not, not anymore. It was the right thing for her."

"And for you?"

"Ah, well." Devan shrugged, looking a bit lost, with a darkness to his eyes she'd never noticed before. Though perhaps she'd been trying not to look too closely... "It was a long time ago."

So not *that* recent. Kate did want to ask him more–but that would be prying, and besides, she was standing in the street, with two increasingly impatient dogs tugging at their leashes, holding a pot of daffodils that would undoubtedly be happier out of the chill. Spring was coming, but it wasn't here yet.

"Well. Thank you for the flowers; they're lovely."

"So are you," he said. Kate could feel her face flushing in response. Devan fell silent a moment, as if he hadn't meant to say that, glancing down. But then he seemed to gather his courage in his hands, because he looked up again, meeting her eyes, and said, "Would you like to have dinner with me sometime? Perhaps leaving the boys at home; they're good lads, but it's not quite warm enough to eat outside yet."

"I–don't know."

"Not a yes...but not a no either. Shall I take heart from that?" Devan said it lightly, but she could tell he was disappointed. He looked like he was about to turn and disappear into his shop. She had to explain.

"It's just–I start chemo on Saturday. Two days. I don't really know how it'll be, so I don't think I should be making dinner plans yet..."

"Ah." His brow furrowed. "Do you have someone to go with you?"

"Oh, don't worry about that." She didn't, but it was fine. Kate would rather do this on her own. "But...I really would like to have dinner with you." They'd told her to live her life, after all, as fully as she could. "Can I call you on Sunday? I should have a better sense of things then." Her heart was racing, and she told it sternly to calm down. It was only dinner.

"I'll be waiting by the phone." His eyes were dark on her, intent. "Good luck with it."

"Thanks. And thanks for these," she said, lifting the little pot in her hand, sending the daffodils, the daffydowndillies, bobbing their heads.

"Anytime, lass." Devan smiled, and then turned, disappearing back into his shop, letting the door closed behind him.

He really couldn't run a business that way.

TORNADO

We knew it would rain today, but
driving to the first chemo appointment,
the radio upgrades the warnings—
thunderstorms, yes, the drops hammer
against the windshield. But hail too,
strong winds, the chance of a tornado.

The garden is waking slowly, early snowdrops
giving way to scilla and chiondoxa,
tiny and tough. With rising warmth, bluebells
and crocus emerge, daffodils open. Cool whites
and blues joined by warmer tones; pink
hyacinths release their scent—
washed away in today's storms.

Some flowers may survive. Others will be beaten
down, petals tattered, leaves and stems dragging
in the mud. Tomorrow I will walk my garden
and count the toll of devastation, mourn each
brave blossom—my hands dug them in,
planted them deep, for this?

But roots survive, the bulbs beneath the soil.
Most daffodils still hold themselves tight-budded,
will open when the sun returns; the tulips
will spring forth, straight and proud and tall.

Into every life a little rain must fall. Last night,
we read over the lists of symptoms and side effects.
No toxins in my soil, but we still pour them
into my body, to fight this strange unwanted growth.

At garden club, I ask, despairing, what to do
about the burdock–I dig and dig, but it keeps
coming back, the bastard. A long taproot, tenacious.

She says even eco-conscious sorts
may resort to poison in the end. But rather
than pouring it over the plant, the soil,
they paint it on, delicately, with a
paintbrush.

The new drugs work like that–focused,
targeted, poisonous effects lessened
and contained. There will still,
undoubtedly, be some damage.

We ask the universe for a favor today.

Let the worst of the storms pass us by,
let the tornado touch down, lightly,
and rise again.
Let the winds dissipate
while there are still flowers on the bud.
Let the sun return.

Five

KATE DIDN'T CALL on Sunday. Devan told himself not to take it personally–the woman surely had enough on her mind, and didn't need him pestering her. And it wasn't even the dinner that was worrying him; he just wanted to know that she was all right. He kept picturing her bright face, faded, lying in a hospital bed. Devan waited through Sunday, through Monday, when the shop was closed. Usually he tried to spend that day deliberately resting, because otherwise it was too easy for the work of the shop to creep into all his waking hours, the fate of the self-employed small business owner. Manju had insisted they spend Mondays together, not working at all. For months after she'd left him, Devan had buried himself in work on that day.

Eventually, time had eased the pain, and Devan had found himself able to sit and read, or watch tv, or putter in the kitchen, though he was an indifferent cook. His parents had both tried to teach him, and Devan could follow a recipe dutifully, but he'd never caught the knack of it. Besides, the grocery store sauces were better than they used to be; he could buy a packet of tikka masala sauce and simmer some chicken in it and it tasted at least a little bit like his mother's. Good enough.

But that Monday, he couldn't concentrate enough for

even that much cooking, and he certainly couldn't read. Devan picked up the latest Sanderson fantasy, a nice thick book to disappear into, but he found himself reading the same page, over and over, until finally he gave up in despair and turned on the tv instead. Television was a little more engaging, especially when he played games on his phone at the same time. Somehow, he got through the day, and then it was Tuesday, time to open the shop again.

She didn't call Tuesday, or come by. Wednesday. Thursday. By Friday, Devan was feeling positively panicked—what if something had gone wrong with that first day of chemo? Kate had said it was routine, that they didn't expect any trouble, but he knew that nothing was certain at a hospital. Things could go wrong in a moment; he'd seen that firsthand. Devan couldn't think on it, winced away from the memory. But as he stripped the thorns from long-stemmed roses, threaded plastic tubes over Gerbera daisy stems, poked wire through the base of the last amaryllis blooms to keep them from splitting, Devan's mind was entirely elsewhere, on the hospital a few miles away, and on her house, just a few blocks distant.

It would be too much to go by. Intrusive, even creepy. But finally Devan gave up and went looking online. Katherine Smith was far too common a name; he couldn't pin one down for certain. But there were three listed as living in Oak Park, with Facebook pages—he sent them all messages, hoping. *Kate? It's Devan from the flower shop. If I've found the right Katherine Smith, let me know how you're doing? I've been fretting.*

Was that too much? At least he'd done something. It might sit in her filtered folder for days or weeks, but surely she'd see it eventually. And in the meantime—it was Friday night. The first Friday of the month, so potluck dinner and board games at Liselle's. Devan would bring flowers as always—an array of tulips this time, classic singles, double-

flowered, fringed, lily-flowered, parrots. The Ottoman
empire had planted tulips to remind them of heaven and
eternal life, but the Dutch considered them a reminder of
how brief life can be instead. Devan had never liked the
Dutch.

Better to focus on the good things in life. Manju had
made stunning trays of tulip petals stuffed with an array of
dips for parties–red pepper & goat cheese, beetroot spread,
salsa verde, spicy hummus. That was all a bit beyond him,
but Devan could toss a few petals into a simple salad;
he liked the sweet crunch of them, and the colors were
striking. Liselle would approve. He'd just have to remind
the group not to try that with store-bought flowers. His
were safe, but the grocery store ones would be risky. Of
course, if any of his friends bought their flowers at the
grocery store, they'd deserve a stern look for it from him.
But probably not an upset stomach.

Devan hoped Kate was feeling all right. She'd write
back to him soon. He was sure of it.

SOLARIZATION

For the first time in two weeks,
I wake up feeling strong. Rested,
with muscles that want to push
themselves out of bed, stretch
to their full extension. Today,
I work the garden. Pull
dandelion and dayflower weeds,
dig burdock, down to the stubborn
taproot. I'll spread clear plastic
and weight it down with bricks,
setting the sun to work, solarizing
the weeds beneath. Six weeks
will ready it for fall planting, for
spinach and chard, lettuce and kale.

Tomorrow is chemo. Six weeks
to go. Tomorrow will set a fire
that will burn through my body,
building to exhaustion, so I wake
only to close my eyes and sleep
again. Cancer is a field of weeds,
and while the battle rages, the
battleground takes a battering.

Six weeks is a long time for ground
to lie unused. All around, other beds
throw off rich harvests. Tomatoes
ripen, peppers bud, the peach tree
has grown heavy with fuzzy fruit.

Still, have faith. This bed will come
to its time again. And maybe, in
some strange ways we cannot yet
predict, will be richer, stronger,
for the long fallow stretch. By fall,
we'll be ready to plant again.
Spinach and chard, lettuce and kale.

Six

WHERE HAD THE days gone? Kate measured her time in chemo appointments crossed off on her calendar, in rooms cleared in the old house. Her progress was slowing. As the online research had warned her, the effects of the chemo were cumulative. The first two treatments hadn't been bad, knocking her out for about a day each, but the later ones had been hitting her harder, taking longer to recover from. She was only about halfway through the second floor rooms, with piles of musty magazines and hoarded newspapers to go. Still, progress was being made.

Kate had finally given up on most of the creaking furniture, had the local resale shop come and take it away, leaving bare rooms with wide-plank wood floors, the dirt of years ground into them. She'd called the LGBT-serving Brown Elephant instead of Goodwill; it made her feel a little better, thinking that her great-uncle's furniture might go to help someone with their healthcare costs. Kate was pretty sure Uncle Robbie had been gay, though he'd never come out to the family about it. He was from the era where you kept such things private, but he'd had a roommate for many years. George had predeceased Rob, and Kate had briefly thought about trying to track down the man's relatives; they probably had as much claim to the house as she did.

But she wouldn't even know where to start; Robbie had kept no memorabilia from their years together—no photos, no letters. Their love, if it had existed, had disappeared into time. Kate's time was disappearing too, her days fading into a haze of exhaustion.

Kate should have called Devan. She'd meant to, but it had somehow been too much. May had slipped away, and most of June too. She been thinking of him—someone who lived in this house had loved irises, because suddenly in June the spiky green-leaved plants all over the neglected yard had suddenly sprouted long stems and a brilliance of blooms. A host of blues, but also yellow and dark purple and magenta and white. It had made her realize how lovely this house must have been, years past, when someone had loved and cared for it.

Had Rob been the iris-lover, or George? Kate would likely never know. She'd almost called Devan's shop, to ask him what irises meant, but instead she'd gone online to find that they were symbols of royalty. They'd also been planted over Greek women's graves, to summon the goddess Iris to guide the dead in their journey.

Kate had closed the laptop then, and called painters instead. They'd be coming next week, to scrape and paint and restore the exterior of the house to its Victorian glory. She'd been too tired to paint out sample colors on boards, so she'd just chosen from the paint chips online, and hoped for the best. Blues and purples, to echo the irises. They'd also been used to make perfume, and as a medicinal remedy. Better uses to dwell on, and she'd made a mental note to ask Devan more about them, some time.

And then Kate had gone back to her dreary work, sorting out what was worth keeping, or donating, or selling, or merely discarding. The rooms were full of dust, and often she only made it through an hour or two before fleeing back downstairs, defeated. At least there was plenty of freelance accounting work to keep her occupied and bolster her bank account, though even that was starting to tire her. Kate would need to take at least a few weeks off soon, but she had enough of a cushion for that. She was spending more and more of her time half-watching re-runs on tv, or staring out the window at the flowers, just letting time pass.

It was only yesterday that she had found the message online from Devan, which had prompted her to finally call, to reassure him that she was all right. Kate was all right–not great, but coping. She would get through this, one way or another. There really wasn't much choice, and only three more chemo appointments to go. Kate really wasn't up to dating, though, and she'd planned to turn Devan down gently when he asked her out. But he'd surprised her. Devan had asked her to dinner tonight, but perhaps wary of scaring her off–smart boy–had emphasized that it was to be a potluck with friends.

She'd almost said no, but he'd been sweet on the phone: *I wouldnae inflict my cooking on you, not to worry, but my friends will put on a bonnie spread.* Devan had been so enthusiastic, Kate hadn't had the heart to tell him that nothing tasted good to her these days. She'd resorted to subsisting mostly on Campbell's chicken-and-stars soup, because she could get it down.

And the next chemo appointment was tomorrow, so she felt as good tonight as she was likely to feel for a while, and they'd said to keep living her life, and this was what people did, they lived their lives and went to dinners and yes, she was standing on the doorstep of his apartment building and she wanted to cry, but buck up, Kate. This was pathetic, and she was not going to just turn around and go back to the old house, even if the dogs would gladly welcome her back. She took a deep breath, resettled the huge bunch of irises in her arm, and reached out to ring the bell.

CHRONIC

It sounds like a dream–to lie in bed
and watch tv, to read and rest. Me at fifteen
would have imagined it heaven, me the girl
who spent summer days in bed, reading
one book after another after another.

It's different, when you have no choice
in the matter. I wake, and feel ill. It's difficult
to get dressed, difficult to come down a flight
of stairs, difficult to make breakfast. One hour
of rest for fifteen minutes of mild exertion.

Somehow, the children are dressed and fed
and even walked to school. Two hours of rest
in exchange. This body is barely functioning.
This body is a betrayal. And even this brain,
normally reliable, is faltering. Is blank.

Entertainment is not entertaining. I have
no heart for wit or laughter, no constitution
for difficult topics. It is all too much. I drift
and wait to get better. Impotent fury simmering
as my life slips away, stolen, moment by day.

Seven

DEVAN HADN'T REALLY expected her to come. Oh, Kate had said she would, but they'd had six months of brief conversations–he had come to expect that that was all they'd ever have. He was in the midst of a round of Boggle when the doorbell rang, and he'd let Jenny get it, intent on trying to come up with at least one or two five-letter words to bolster his score. So he missed the moment when she came into his apartment, only raising his eyes when the timer went off, signaling the end of the round.

"Kate!" He'd risen and gone to her then, taking the irises out of her hand. "Well, these are gorgeous, aren't they?" She, on the other hand, wasn't looking well. Her hair had thinned, and her face looked more gaunt than it had seven weeks ago. Devan wanted to reach out, touch her cheek, reassure himself that the bones would still be solid under his touch. But he could just imagine what the dozen people crowded into his living room would think if he did that, not to mention the girl herself, so Devan refrained, contenting himself with saying, "It's good to see you."

She smiled up at him, but then looked around the room, seeming a bit bewildered. "You have a lot of...friends."

Devan laughed, guessing what she had wanted to say. He could see the apartment through her eyes, jam-packed as it was with all the stuff Manju had left behind. Rugs and pillows and paintings, too many end tables and comfy chairs. His wife had walked out of her old life with nothing but the clothes on her back—well, that and a decent bank account from her half of the house sale. She'd said she wanted to start over, wanted to travel the world with nothing but what she could carry on her back.

After what she'd been through, Devan couldn't blame Manju for wanting to leave painful memories behind. He kept meaning to dispose of at least some of the things that had filled their little house and was now much too much for this even smaller apartment, especially when it was also crammed full of people, as it was tonight, on his turn to host game night. Devan pitched his voice louder than normal, to cut above the noise of the crowd. "Try not to trip over anything. I'll introduce you to this lot later—" Tess and Tish had already started another Boggle round without him, and the others were setting up in teams for a game of Encore, which would be easy enough for them to join into in a bit. "Let's put these in water, and get you something to eat."

"I'm really not hungry," Kate protested faintly. She looked like she wanted to flee from the noise, the crowd, but thankfully, she followed him into the kitchen. Three more people in here, barely standing room, but Devan managed to reach down a vase for the flowers—mostly iris Pallida Dalmatica, the classic perfume iris, but with a nice selection of others: Florentina, Wabash, Queen of May, plus a few he didn't recognize. Where had she found them? He didn't sell these varieties in his shop...

"You must be Kate," Jenny said. She'd followed them into the kitchen, and was now reaching down a glass for her. "Dev's been talking about you for months, but we were despairing that we'd ever get to meet you."

Had he really? Jenny was his oldest friend, and she'd

know if anyone would–she was the one he confided in, the one who'd stood by him through the dark time after the loss, after Manju left. Had he really been talking about Kate that much? Devan supposed he must have been. Jenny continued, "What will you drink? We have wine, beer, cider, soda, juice, and, of course, Scotch. He likes the peaty ones, and plenty of them, ugh, but there's some Macallan if you'd rather."

"Just water for me, thanks." Kate said. She looked a little pale. "I'm not much of a drinker."

Devan asked, "Is the crowd too much for you? Here–" he pushed past Linwood and Tansy, who were, as usual, too busy making out to really notice, opening the door off the kitchen to the back balcony. "It's quieter out here."

Kate followed him out; Jenny, with a knowing glint in her eye, smiled and turned back to the main room. Devan let the door shut behind them, cutting the noise of the party down to a dull roar.

There wasn't much room on this balcony, crowded as it was with various pots holding a host of little experiments. He'd been lucky, to find a place with a south-facing balcony. But maybe Devan should've thought to leave a little space for chairs, or at least a little more standing room.

Kate said, "Your friends seem nice."

He smiled. "They can be a little overbearing, but they mean well. You have to forgive Jenny–she's known me a long time."

"It must be nice to have so many people who want to spend time with you."

His eyebrow rose, of its own volition. "You say that like you don't." Devan couldn't imagine that she wouldn't have a host of friends of her own–her light was dimmed a little right now, but he was sure that in other circumstances, Kate would shine.

"Oh, well," she said, uncertainly. "I had plenty of friends in New York, but I'm still new here. And–" Kate raised her hand almost to her hair in an unconscious gesture, then let it fall again. "I'm not the best company these days."

"I beg to differ," Devan said, as gently as he could. He wanted to say or do—something, he wasn't sure what exactly. Something that would erase the sad, lost look in her eyes. "How are the treatments going?"

"Oh, well enough. Chemo is pretty much exactly as they say it is—well, the anti-nausea meds are much better than they used to be, so that's something." She sipped at her glass of water. "That's actually quite a lot."

"I'm glad for that." What he wanted to do was kiss her. Reach down to her chin, tilt her head up a little, and press a kiss against those lips that, Devan was coming to realize, he had been wanting to kiss for months. Jenny was right—this had been going on for quite a while. Maybe since the first day Kate had walked into his shop? But the woman was sick, vulnerable—it would be unfair to press her now. So he did nothing, and the silence between them lengthened, until finally she spoke.

"Tomorrow's my birthday," she said.

"Well. Happy birthday." Surely reason enough for a birthday kiss? No.

"I'm going to be thirty-two. That's not so old."

"No, it's not old at all. I'm thirty-nine myself."

"But there's a good chance I won't be able to get pregnant after the chemo." She shrugged. "The doctors recommended I freeze some eggs, so I did. It'll probably be all right. But I don't really know. I don't even know if I want kids."

"Ah." And he should say something comforting, something appropriate, but the words had frozen in his throat, as if he'd swallowed a cube of ice. Devan could use another drink, or several. The Laphroig was on the counter, just on the other side of the door.

She shook her head sharply, as if dashing away dark thoughts. "I'm sorry—this is too much. I barely know you.

There's just...a lot on my mind these days."

He swallowed, and managed to get out a few words. "No, it's all right. " One word in front of the other, that was the ticket. "And the whole point of your coming by was to get to know me better, right?" Devan even managed to pull off a smile.

"Right," she said, smiling faintly in return.

"Well, if you think you can stand my raucous friends, let's see if we can make it past the two making out shamelessly in my kitchen." Sounds of singing were coming faintly through the door–they must have started the game of Encore. "Do you sing?"

Her brow furrowed. "Sing? I like musicals, but I don't really have a good voice. Mostly, I sing in the shower."

Devan closed his eyes against a sudden vision of what Kate might look like, entirely undressed in his shower. Not now, boy. "Well, then, you'll fit right in. Most of us sound like we're murdering cats, but we have fun anyway."

"Fun," she said, the word sounding oddly alien on her tongue. "Okay–let's have some fun." And if there was more determination than lightness in her tone, at least she was here, and not bolting out the door. Devan would take what he could get, for now.

Many Happy Returns

Last February, my doctor called,
her voice shaken as she told me
I had cancer. Not an oncologist,
not the sort of news she often
delivers, and to one so relatively
young. It was a few days, or maybe
weeks–everything blurs already --
before they gave me a prognosis.
They'd caught it early, the dice roll
in my favor, everything would
(probably) be fine.

So here we are, halfway through
a year of treatment, disease
mostly gone. From this point on,
it's prophylactic, searching for any
microcancers, waging war against
the possibility of recurrence. Let us
starve and poison the beast, let us
cut and burn the ground, denying
it re-entry. That's the hope.

My birthday, and the kind wishes
are pouring in. Hopes for many
happy returns, and I'm grateful,
remembering that February day,
the cold wind sleeting outside
my office. I sat alone with the news,
waiting until I had stopped shaking
enough to drive safely home.

That day, I did not know if I
would live to see this birthday.
Cancer is the second leading
cause of death in America, right
after heart disease. One or the
other will likely get me, get you,
in the end. This is what it is
to have a birthday–we come
with expiration dates as well.

All we can hope is that between
beginning and end, there lives
a great exuberance–of friends
and family, love and laughter,
balloons and presents and cake.

Eight

THE DOORBELL RANG, echoing through the first floor and startling Kate. It wasn't a sound she was used to hearing. The dogs started barking furiously, running up and down the hall. Maybe a package? Her mother had sent a carton of ginger things last week–gingerbread, ginger cookies, ginger tea, and some straight up ginger–and Kate knew the woman meant well, but the smell of it had nauseated her before she even finished opening the box. Ginger might help other people, and normally she loved it, especially crystallized and added to a nice shortbread cookie. But she couldn't stand it now; she'd added it to the long list of food aversions. Kate hadn't been eating much lately, and had lost five pounds in the last few weeks.

If the chemo were a longer course of treatment, that might become a problem, but she was almost done now, just one more treatment to go. Her mother would be irritatingly pleased by the weight loss, would pinch her cheek if allowed. She wouldn't like the lack of hair, though. It was falling out faster, and if hadn't been thick to begin with, Kate probably would've shaved it by now. Maybe next week; it seemed like a lot of work. *Ring! Ring!* Right, the doorbell. *Bark bark bark!!!* Cinnamon was going nuts.

Kate supposed she should get that, but getting up off

the couch was appallingly hard. She loved this couch and hated it at the same time; she mostly slept on it now, rather than fighting the stairs. It was the last big piece of furniture left from her great-uncle. When this was all over, she was going to burn this couch. It could go up in a wood-and-red-velvet fire—her uncle had had rather medieval tastes.

She probably wouldn't actually burn it. But Kate was definitely buying herself a new couch. Someone else would love this one, someone who hadn't practically melded with it over the last few months. *Ring! Bark!* Dammit. The delivery person must need a signature for whatever stupid thing her mother had sent her now. Before the gingerbread, it had been a pile of warm woolly hats (which wouldn't be needed for months, if at all), and before that, a stack of cancer memoirs—a reasonable idea, but it turned out the last thing Kate wanted to do was read about someone else's experience of cancer. *Ring!* Cursing, Kate swung her legs off the couch. That was much harder than it ought to be.

It took her three rings to make it all the way down the hall to the front door, pushing past the over-excited dogs, and Devan's worried face through the glass didn't cheer her as it ought. He looked much too good, in a crisp white shirt and blue jeans, his skin gone brown with the end of summer. Gardeners got plenty of time outside, she supposed. Whereas she had turned into something you might find in a dark cavern, fish-belly pale, with sunken cheeks and probably terrible breath—she hadn't bothered to brush her teeth in days. Or shower, for that matter—showering was depressing; too much hair came off every time.

Why was he even here? She'd had a nice enough time at his party, and they'd even had lunch a few days later. But then she'd started to get so tired, and had begun making excuses to avoid going out. Now she had turned into a troll. Why didn't Devan take one look at her, and flee in terror?

Kate opened the door, realizing as she did that his friend

Jenny was a few steps to the side, waiting with him. "Hello."

Devan said, his tone apologetic, "You haven't been picking up your phone, or responding to my messages. I got worried."

"I'm sorry." She found herself leaning against the doorframe, and hoped they didn't notice.

He raised a protesting hand. "No, dinnae be sorry, lass. You have every right not to respond, and if you'd rather we went away, we'll do that right now—just say the word. I just wanted to be sure nothing had happened."

She shook her head. "No, nothing's happened. I'm fine, or at least, as well as can be expected right now. Everything's progressing as it should. I'd invite you in, but the place is a disaster."

Jenny chirped up, "We don't care about that, love. But surely you're not trying to keep it up on your own?"

Kate raised an eyebrow. *That* didn't take too much energy. "Well, I live alone."

The other woman frowned, making her no less pretty. Her sleek brown hair was neatly cut into a sleek cap that framed her face, and bright blue eyes glinted from a sweetly-rounded face. She looked like a bird, one of the charming little brown birds that had flocked to the feeders, back when Kate had still had the energy to fill them. Why was Devan still here, when he could be off doing something with someone as lovely as Jenny?

Jenny, of course, had no idea what was rolling through Kate's head, and continued on, "But there's a service that comes and cleans for women who have cancer—oh, don't you remember, Dev, when my aunt got breast cancer, they came every week. And there were the casserole delivering women...if you'd like a tray of mac-and-cheese, it'd be on your doorstep tomorrow." Jenny tactfully didn't say anything about how Kate looked like she could use a good meal or several. "And there's another organization that'll give you rides to the hospital when you need them–you haven't been trying to drive yourself, have you?"

"No–I've been taking cabs for the last month." Since she'd found herself dozing off at the wheel once, and scared herself silly. Kate's financial cushion was disappearing faster than she'd hoped, since she really hadn't been able to work in weeks, falling asleep every time she tried. It had been worrying her; she always liked to have several months' buffer, just in case. If her inability to work went on much longer, Kate would start eating into the money she'd set aside to start her new business, and that would really break her heart. "I didn't know." She felt stupid. Maybe if Kate had read those books her mother had sent, she would have known about such things.

"Let us in, Katie." Devan's voice was gentle, and his deep brown eyes entreating. "We can at least do a round of dishes for you. And maybe you'd let me tie up those rose canes, before they poke the poor doggies' eyes out?"

Oh, the kitchen was too disgusting, dishes piled high, counters covered in plates crusted with food she had barely tasted before discarding. It was embarrassing; she couldn't. Her first guests in this house–they deserved better than this. Her mother would be appalled.

But he'd called her Katie. Her dad had called her that, when she was small. It was probably the exhaustion that brought tears pricking to her eyes, that let Kate step back, opening the way.

The words were quiet, almost a sigh. But loud enough to be heard. "All right then. Come in."

What Happens In The Dark

Each round of chemo
is followed by a smothering;
mind quieted, reduced to
enduring, waiting. Uncaring.

Eventually, it wakes again
and it is almost too much.
Thought after thought after
thought, connections exploding.

As the next round approaches,
the intensity impossibly increases.
Chain lightning, racing across
vast fields, as dusk settles.

Nine

ONLY A FEW weeks since she'd first let him into her house—let them both in, Devan and Jenny. Jenny had taken one look at the disaster of a kitchen, pronounced, "Mine," and shoved him out again. After so many years of friendship, he'd known better than to argue, and he'd never much liked washing up anyway. But Devan could give the first floor a good sweeping out, and had done so, over Kate's protest that it wasn't necessary, that she wasn't some damsel in distress. She damn well was in distress, and no shame in that. The measure of the truth of it was that after one feeble protest, she'd stopped trying to stop him, and had gone back to lying down on the couch. By the time he'd finished sweeping up, Kate was fast asleep, and Devan had resisted the urge to brush sweaty curls away from her forehead. He'd gone to go help Jenny in the kitchen instead—the floor needed a good mopping.

That visit was the first of many—Kate had actually called him the next day, asked if Devan would mind taking the dogs on a walk. They were getting bored with just running around the back yard. He'd jumped at the request, and after a few days of dog-walking, she'd deigned to let him start clearing the garden—nothing too dramatic, just taking care of the worst of it so that the Village didn't slap her with a hefty fine. *He* liked the gone-wild look, but there were ordinances meant to keep the rodents and other small animals out. Devan was pretty sure Kate had rabbits, though—it was amazing they'd survived the dogs. *Fast* bunnies—his father, who had taken him as a child to see the wild rabbits on Edinburgh's castle hillside, would have approved.

His da would approve of Kate too, Devan thought, though it was actually a little hard to say why. She wasn't the life of the party, not the way Manju had been. Kate was quiet much of the time, but had a sharp wit; she'd occasionally drop a funny line that he only got minutes (or hours) later. But that wasn't the only thing Devan liked about her. He liked Kate's honesty, and the forthright way she was approaching this illness, and how strong she clearly was—and he loved the way she looked at him, when she thought he wasn't looking. It had been a long time since a woman had looked at him like that.

Three weeks, and the requests for help had gotten more serious, which he took as the greatest of compliments. This morning she'd asked if he'd drive her to her upcoming lumpectomy appointment, and stay, and drive her back after. Her mother had offered to come, but Kate said that would be harder than doing it alone, and her best friend from New York, who *would* be coming out, apparently didn't drive. He'd agreed, of course—he could get Linwood to cover the shop for the day. And then she'd asked him if he could stop by later today. She hadn't said why, and he hadn't asked. Whatever he could do for her, he would.

He rang the bell, rousing the predictable chorus of barking dogs. When she opened the door, the dogs surged out, almost knocking him over. It was almost enough to keep him from noticing what she held in her hand—until she held it out to him. An electric razor.

"It's time," Kate said quietly. "I thought I could just do

it myself, but I–I'd just rather not." Her voice was shaky, as if she balanced on a ragged edge. "If it's too much..."

"No, of course not." Devan reached out to take the razor from her, but found himself wrapping his hand around hers instead, the razor awkwardly clasped within their joint grasp. It only lasted for a moment, but the contact sent a shiver racing through him, set his pulse racing. Then Devan took the razor, letting her hand drop away.

"We can do it in the kitchen," Kate said. She laughed, or tried to. It sounded more than a little forced. "I just hope I have a nice-shaped head. You never know. I could end up looking like a cauliflower, all bumpy."

"I like cauliflower curry," Devan said. "My mother makes it with raisins, which sounds disgusting, but is actually delicious."

Kate laughed again, this time with more lightness in the sound. "That's often the way with raisins," she said. She turned, heading back into the house, and he followed her inside, letting the door close behind him. "When all this is over, I'll make you my raisin shortbread. It's a revelation."

Good. She was looking forward, picturing a day when all this would be over. That was a trend that should be encouraged. Tomorrow, Devan would bring her bulb catalogs; September was the perfect time to order bulbs for autumn planting. This garden would look splendid, covered in a carpet of tiny blue scilla come spring, with white Thalia daffodils to follow, perennials that would come back year after year. He just hoped she'd still want him around in the spring, when all this was over.

CURED

The news is met with great rejoicing
as it should be, yet the ringing exultations
come muffled. Was the danger ever truly felt?
Now the rush of death's wings has apparently
passed by, there should be a stronger sense
of triumph. Relief, yes. Their shared happiness
helps, adds a note of celebration to the news,
and yet. The cure is–attenuated. If cured,
should we not be done with taking medicine?

Yet the treatments drag on, small jabs
and aches, the stripping down and twisting
this way and that on command, a thousand
small indignities. Not as upsetting to me
as to many, and yet, it would be better
to be done with them. There are days
when the presence of the port beneath
the skin of my chest, hard foreign presence,
the visible, palpable tube leading from it
to a beating vein, feels an intrusion
past bearing, and if nails were sharp enough,
one might be tempted to rip it out. One might
dream of that furious tearing. My nails
are soft, damaged, quick to break,
darkened still, though hands and feet finally
have returned to their accustomed hue.
The line of pale pink creeps slowly forward
along the nail, a promise of returning health
but damnably slow. It doesn't matter.

Only cosmetic, and yet. The scar of the port
is a thin fading line; the scar of lymph surgery
will soon be the same, but the breast–oh.
There's a gash, there's a jagged river cutting
canyons through remaining flesh. Shapely
enough in clothes–disguise, but brace to stare
naked in the mirror at undeniable truth–
this is ugly, this scar, this breast. They were
never picture perfect, but once, they were
pleasant enough to look upon, once, they
were photographed, but it's too soon
to look at those photos again, to confront
what once was. It doesn't matter much.

Not compared to the greater losses, the
nipple that no longer works, nerves cut,
the eggs that have stopped releasing–and
although we were done with them, and it's
a relief, practically speaking, still, a loss,
a loss. Worst of all, the hours gone. Should
be grateful we didn't lose them all; friends have,
their time cut brutally short. Should rejoice.

Someday I shall. Now, the bells are muffled,
now the ongoing demands, the losses
roll over me in waves, and all I can do:
roll with them, waiting for the better day to come.

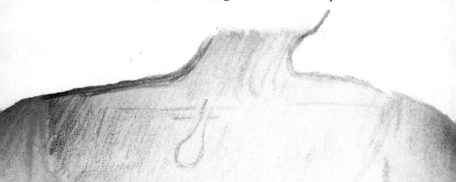

Ten

"DAMMIT!" KATE HAD dropped one of the heavy metal rods on her toe, and now she was hopping around, cursing as if it would help. "Dammit, dammit, dammit!" She'd never been particularly good at cursing; a moment like this probably deserved something more creative, but this was the best she could do. Her best was clearly not good enough.

The problem was that Kate had tried to put the rack together on her own. The picture clearly showed two people assembling the metal rack, but she'd been sure she could manage it by herself. And normally, she probably could, but the surgery site was still healing, and while Kate was off the painkillers completely now and generally felt fine, if she pushed or pulled a little too hard or in the wrong direction, her body immediately reminded her that it was not fully healed, and wouldn't be for some time to come. That was how she'd ended up dropping the rod on her foot, adding insult to injury.

Su Lin had been a huge help last week, and a tremendous comfort too–surviving four years of boarding school bonded best girlfriends, probably for life. She'd jumped at the chance to come out and help after the surgery, and had scolded Kate for not calling her sooner. But after a week, she hadn't been able to take any more time off work, so Kate had said a sad goodbye and sent her back to her husband in Santa Fe. And then Kate was on her own again. She should just go upstairs and call Devan or Jenny, see if one of them was available to come help out. She would, in a minute. Although she really *ought* to be able to do this on her own...

The dogs burst into frenzied barking, drowning out what must be the doorbell ringing upstairs. Ugh–it was going to take a while to weave her way through the mess of cardboard boxes and packaging strewn across the basement. She hoped whomever it was would wait. The dogs' barking was growing even louder, if that were possible. Kate felt her heart race a bit–what was bothering them?

"Kate?" His voice echoed faintly down the back stairs.

"Devan?" Oddly, her heart seemed to be going even faster now. Ba-dump, ba-dump, ba-dump! "I'm in the basement–come down!"

His voice echoed down the stairs. "Kate, I'm sorry to just walk in like this, but Jenny was fretting that you wouldn't be able to cook yet, so she made you a lasagna and I didn't want to just leave it outside, so I brought it into the kitchen–you really ought to lock your front door–and I thought you might like some of the first crop of dahlias– Jesus wept. What *is* all this?" Devan had stopped at the base of the stairs, a massive array of glorious flowers cradled in his arms, and was looking around in bewilderment. It wasn't kind to laugh at him, so Kate stifled the chuckle rising in her throat, trying to focus instead on the flowers in his arms. So many shapes and such bright colors! Kate was itching to draw them, which was a much better focus for her than Devan's reaction to her basement. After all, it was a bizarre sight if you weren't expecting it.

The space had first been completely cleared and cleaned, and now she was setting up her racks, which would support bins holding her paints, fabric, and printing supplies. All of the materials were in stacked plastic bins lined up neatly along the stone walls, safe from water and animals, but she was dying to get them out, get her hands on fabric again. When Kate had first moved here, the place was such a disaster that she hadn't even tried to unpack her supplies. It was far too filthy to risk opening the bins.

And then, well, cancer, which had eaten up far more hours than she'd expected, in doctor visits and sheer exhaustion. All the spare hours that she'd meant to put towards her work had disappeared into the hospital instead—she'd lost almost a year already, and if Kate stopped to think about that, she could feel the simmering fury rising, like lava on volcano day. She'd kept sketching—that was something. Kate had been uploading designs to Spoonflower off and on, which was great for getting audience feedback and even provided a small income stream. The real money would come with a proper fabric line, of course. That was the goal. Kate had kept the blog updated with the designs and her treatments, so she hadn't lost too much ground. She had a whole fairy tale line planned out, for her first serious print run, and all she needed to do was actually start printing...

"I thought you were an accountant!" Devan said. There was a faint hint of accusation in his voice, as if she'd betrayed him somehow. Odd.

Kate shrugged. "Well, accounting paid the bills. It's what let me save up enough that I could afford to start doing what I really wanted—I spent the last three years taking night and weekend classes, studying drawing and design." She hesitated, then said firmly, "I'm going to be a fabric designer." Had she ever said it out loud before? Did she dare to let that dream out into the world, words trembling in the air, turning real?

Devan frowned. "You should be careful, Kate. It's not easy, starting your own business. Most new businesses fail, you know."

"I've done my research and crunched the numbers," Kate said, oddly disappointed. Did Devan think so poorly of her, of her abilities? He hadn't seen her work, of course, but to just assume she couldn't do it... Her stomach seemed to be twisting into knots.

Devan took a step towards her, so they were separated only by the length of a cardboard packing box. "I'd just hate to see you go down, lass, after all you've been through, all you've fought for."

"I'm going to be fine," she said, flatly. She was—she knew that. Kate was tired right now, and she still had six weeks of radiation coming, before this course of treatment would be done. But she was going to get her life back—she was determined to do so. And when she did, she'd be going after her dreams with both hands, no matter what Devan McLeod had to say about it. "I really ought to get back to this—"

"Can I help?"

And for a moment, she wanted to say no, to punish Devan for his lack of enthusiasm. But that was foolish, and petty too. Kate took a deep breath, let the irritation wash away. Devan hadn't even seen her work, after all. Once he did, then he'd understand. But first, she had six racks to assemble... "A little help would be great. Thank you."

"Let me just get these in water, then, and I'll be right back." He paused, and then said shyly, "Dahlias are supposed to symbolize grace under pressure, especially in challenging situations. They made me think of you." And before Kate could respond, Devan was ducking back up the stairs, his lanky form disappearing. Well, when he went and said a thing like that, how could a girl stay mad?

The Bath

Baths have been forbidden
for ten days. Showers permitted
not long after surgery, but
baths were taboo, proscribed,
verboten. Unsure what to do
with this sudden wealth, first
there was reading. The prose
unremarkable, but the story
gripping. Then, watching
a show, while tending to feet
darkened by chemo (hyper-
pigmentation, it's called) and
by garden soil that found its way
past flimsy shoe barriers.
Soaking and pumicing and
sugar scrub, and now these
feet are soft and smooth,
ready for kisses, should any
be offered. The bald scalp
has been washed as well,
dried and lotioned, and now
the faint trace of stubble has
a fuzzy halo, inviting touch.
Showers are refreshing, but
baths are seductive. Tonight,
maybe another bath, maybe
with wine and chocolates. I
will wrinkle into a raisin; you
will know me by my wrinkles,
soft and numerous and lush.

Eleven

KNOCKING AT THE door, which Devan would ignore, as he'd ignored all the knockings beforehand–he'd closed the shop, dammit. Couldn't the fools read the sign? But this just kept going and going, accompanied now by barking, and gods, Devan knew those dogs. What was Kate doing here? Couldn't she just leave him alone?

She didn't seem to be going away. Finally, Devan dragged himself out of the battered old rolling chair in the back room– it wasn't comfortable anyway. He should just go home, though he didn't want to be home, home was worse. He should get a comfortable chair for the office, a proper misery chair that he could sink into, a nice leather recliner like his da had in his study. Not that Devan could afford a chair like that.

He opened the door, setting the bell jingling and sending the dogs into a frenzy. "Dammit, Katie."

She frowned up at him. "I'm the one getting irradiated every day, but you're the one who looks terrible."

"Did you come by to compliment me, then?"

"Are you going to let me in? It's freezing."

It had been a nasty November so far–an early hard frost that killed the dahlias and blackened the remaining autumn foliage. Pumpkins rotting on the vine, pansies quickly gone to shriveled dust. No snow to pretty the place up–just grey skies and drippy rain that got into your boots and your bones. It suited Devan's mood, but had killed foot traffic in the village; business had been terrible, and even the usual spike of women buying their Thanksgiving décor had been much smaller than usual. Devan had been relying on that and the Christmas rush to get him over this hump, but the last few weeks sales had been so grim that he'd finally forced himself to look at the accounts he'd been avoiding. Numbers could be cruel.

"Come in, if you want." It didn't matter.

Kate hesitated. "The dogs..."

"Oh, they can come in too. I dinnae care."

She came in then, bringing the beasts with her, letting the door clang shut on the chill wind and barren sky. Barren, ah, that was the word. His da would've been proud of him for coming up with that one, a nice poetic word. Of course, Amma would have scolded him if he'd dared say it out loud; Manju hadn't actually been barren, of course. They'd just had bad luck, the worst of luck. Christmas would be here soon, a child is born...theirs had been born, and been lost soon thereafter. And then he'd lost his wife as well, let her walk out the door, away from him. She was happy now, finally. That was something. All he'd had left was the shop, and now...

Kate followed him down the hall, scolding. "This is the third time I've come by this week—you haven't picked up the phone, answered my messages. And the shop is closed when it's supposed to be open."

He shrugged. "I'm cutting back."

"Why? I'd think you'd be in the midst of holiday rush right now..."

"Can't afford the extra help." Devan had finally reached the dimly-lit back office and his desk again; he slumped into the rolling chair, reached for the ready glass. He'd just poured another slug, and it was waiting for him, golden and seductive, promising to carry him far, far away from this miserable place.

"Devan. Dev! What the hell is going on?" Kate was standing too close, he could smell the scent of her, even though she was still bundled up in coat and scarf and hat, just that small face peeping out, bewildered and concerned. Devan was sick of seeing concern on the faces of his friends.

"It's just...a bad week. Old ghosts come back to haunt me, this time of year."

She looked like she wanted to press, but didn't. Let Devan knock back the whiskey, let the warmth pool in his belly. Just stood there, silent, until he felt compelled to speak again.

"As for the shop, well." It was embarrassing to admit, but what did he have to lose, really? "I've gotten myself into a wee bit of trouble with the tax man, you see. I'll likely have to give the whole thing up."

She frowned. "But you love this store."

"You can't always keep the things you love."

"Maybe not," Kate said, slowly. "But you can damn well try. You can fight for it."

Devan laughed shortly. "Ah. You're the fighter, not me. I've seen you, fighting all this last year, month after month. You're going to beat this thing, it's clear. You'll get your fabric business up and running too, and clear your uncle's house, and plant your garden. All good things will come to you. As for me–I'll be fine. I do better this way, alone in the dark."

"But–"

"Leave it, Kate!" he snapped. And regretted it a little, seeing the hurt on her face, but the whiskey had numbed him too, and it was easier just to close his eyes than be forced to face what he'd done.

It was quiet for a long moment, and then she said, "Fine." And then she was turning, walking away and taking her dogs with her, out the door and presumably out of his life. Devan's chest ached with the pain of it, but it was also felt right. This was what he deserved, because he'd messed up–he hadn't been able to love his wife enough to make up for their loss, to make Manju happy. After she'd left, he'd paid attention to his plants, but not to the books, and now Devan was going to lose the store too. Everything he'd ever wanted was slipping through his fingers, and worst of all, he deserved it.

He turned out the small desk lamp, leaving him truly in the dark. He didn't even want another drink; it didn't really help. In the old days, he would turn to the garden for solace, digging his fingers into rich soil. Devan should be potting up bulbs for forcing now, looking ahead to the spring to come. But he had no heart for forcing anything anymore. He would just sit.

Eventually, it'd be late enough to go to sleep.

TERRAIN

My body has come to resemble
a distant planet
deep fissures, scarred peaks,
strange shadings of light
and dark. The skin still peeling,
slower now, changing day
to day. Beneath the surface,
adhesions: fibrous bands that
form between tissues, a type
of invisible scarring. Invisible,
but palpable. I can't bear
to look for long, change hastily,
eyes averted. In the shower,
soap quickly, rinse with as little
touch as possible. I should massage
the adhesions, so they will break
down sooner. I should spread
lotion on the skin, to minimize
scarring. The more care I take now,
the faster the healing process
will go, or so I'm told. Instead,
I look away, and wait for time
to do its job. I take photos
for documentation, because I
am a writer, this is my job.
I throw them away, too ugly
to post, to inflict on others, except
for one, abstracted enough
to pass for some strange
lunar surface. An image sent
back to the humans, from
a lonely far traveller
on a cold shore.

Twelve

THE HARDEST PART was the first step, the initial phone call to Jenny. Who was Kate, after all, to interfere? But in the end, she couldn't let Devan just sink into his misery like that, drown in the swamp of it. So Kate went online and found Jenny's e-mail and asked if she could call and Jenny said yes. That started off a flurry of phone calls, and then conversations with semi-strangers around Kate's dining table, but these people didn't feel like strangers, united as they were in their concern for Devan, their eagerness to help.

Jenny had gotten a spare key from Linwood. They'd snuck in late at night and stayed up working for hours, until the dawn light was breaking and they were exhausted and giddy with it–though the wine probably helped with the giddiness. Jenny, it turned out, had a wicked sense of humor and a fondness for bawdy old drinking songs–what did the Scotsman have under his kilt? Kate thought she might quite like to find out. And the look in Devan's eyes when he walked in the next morning, seeing the whole crew waiting for him, seeing what they had wrought, was only matched by the look on his face now, just a few weeks later.

"I didn't think you could do it." Devan stood in the midst of his ravaged store. December 24th, Christmas Eve, and the shelves were almost empty, stripped of potted amaryllises, paperwhites, Christmas and Hanukkah décor. Mistletoe kissing balls and front door wreaths, coils of garland greenery and sleigh centerpieces. Pine swags and rosemary topiaries, little calamondin orange trees and night-blooming jasmine, and the poinsettias–all the poinsettias in pink and red and white and striped. And Kate's drawings brightening the room further, tucked in here and there, charming pencil sketches of colorful flowers, presented in little brass frames. All gone. The store was devastated, down to its last few ornaments, a glitter of silver tinsel and gold balls. "How in the world did you sell it all?"

"It wasn't just me," Kate protested, though the tone of satisfaction in her voice belied her words. She looked around the space, taking it in. Fairy lights lit the dusk; Jenny had organized that, bringing in strand after strand to decorate the windows, walls, even the ceiling, making magic. The last of the crowd had left a few minutes before, heading off to their family celebrations of the holiday, leaving the two of them alone in the store. "Your friends are the ones who deserve the credit–the three-week holiday extravaganza they put on definitely drew in the crowds. Carolers and recorder consorts playing medieval music, the solstice candle ceremony, nightly story readings. Fruitcake and cookies and holiday wassail. Tess made a perfect Santa. And of course, you're the one who stocked the store, who provided all these lovely items for them to sell."

Devan shook his head. "I didn't even have to put them on sale, though. Full price–I still can't believe you got so many people to pay full price!"

Kate cocked her head, looking up at him, her gaze serious and steady. "So, here's the million-dollar question– is it enough?"

"Enough to pay the tax man? Well, it won't cover the entire bill," Devan admitted, abashedly. He never should have let things get that bad, or indulged his black streak so when he finally faced the truth. "But I spent a while on the phone with them yesterday–they're willing to work with me, set out a repayment schedule that should be manageable. This–this is going to make it possible. Kate, I don't know how to thank you." Last month, he wouldn't have even cared, but day after day of his friends rallying around, filling him with cookies and cheer, had somehow lifted the dark mood from him.

Probably not forever–Devan had been prone to that sort of grey funk his entire life, and even a three-week party with his friends wasn't going to cure that. But next time he felt the shadows coming on, maybe he would do something about them. Manju had always been trying to get him to go talk to someone. Devan hadn't been ready to listen back then.

Kate smiled. "Well, you can thank me by not getting into this sort of situation again. Pay your bills on time, so you don't get hit with any more late fees. It hurts my black accountant's heart to think of you giving the IRS more money than you have to."

"Yes, ma'am," Devan said, laughing. "Although I'm not sure I believe you really have an accountant's heart." Her smile lit her face–Kate was looking so much better now, with the last of the treatment finally done. Oh, there'd be follow-up for another year, but the worst of it had passed. Worth celebrating. "That seems a cold thing, a place for adding and subtracting and measuring out due weight. From what I know of you, I can't believe your heart is so dry and sad." He shifted a little closer to her, noting that she didn't move away.

"It's not feeling sad, I admit." She grinned, a smile of pure satisfaction. "Right now, I feel like it could light up the room, all by itself. It feels like everything is possible, right now, like I can do anything I set my mind to. Is that too smug?"

"Sounds just exactly smug enough. I just hope I'm around to see what you set yourself to doing next year." Was it too daring, to bend down and kiss her now? There was no mistletoe to provide an excuse–they'd sold it all.

"I'd like that," Kate said softly. And then she was stepping forward, raising up on tiptoes, so it seemed like it wasn't too daring at all. So Devan bent down and kissed her, there in the gorgeous wasteland they'd created, amidst the fallen pine needles that would need sweeping up. Tomorrow, or possibly the day after.

Right now, he was kissing Kate, and everything else could wait.

SNOWDROP IN MARCH

The first snowdrops appeared
weeks ago, pushing through hard ground,
improbably delicate, yet strong enough
to survive cutting wind, the kind
that knifes through to bone
no matter how many layers you
pile on. Winters in Chicago
are long, even now, after climate
change has hastened safe
planting dates, shifted zones
thrown time out of joint. March still
brings snowdrops and impatience.

Why must I wait for scilla, crocuses,
chionodoxa, striped squill, reticulated
irises? All the little bulbs, early
bloomers that many wouldn't
bother with, but I love them best
because winter is long and cold
and hard and nothing feels as good
as forsythia finally exploding.
I don't even like yellow.

Last year's cancer was long and hard
as a Chicago winter, the way
our winters used to be, when cold grey
slush crept into your boot tops, as you
dug your car out from its city spot,
hours to get it free, and you threw
a lawn chair in the space and hoped
it'd be waiting when you finally came home

in the dark. If you have to shovel out
one more damned spot, you might cry.

Last year lasted too long, and now
impatience bites at my chapped
heels. I am behind on everything
and the ground is still frozen solid
and it is no use trying to dig here,
to sow seed. The roots are still
sleeping, soaking up the slow-
emerging sun. Snowdrops herald
brighter days to come, but now
we play a waiting game.

Tender transplants must be hardened
off, in sheltered spots, a few hours
more each time. A slow accretion,
or they will succumb to the ravages
of wind and even sun. Pace yourself.
Healing has its own schedule; though
you can't see it, day by day the green
tips rise, buds ripen, soon to unfurl.

*****

MARY ANNE MOHANRAJ wrote *Bodies in Motion* (finalist for the Asian American Book Awards) and twelve other titles. She is Clinical Associate Professor of fiction and literature at the University of Illinois at Chicago, and serves as a Trustee of the Oak Park Library. Her most recent books are *The Stars Change* (science fiction) and *A Feast of Serendib* (a Sri Lankan cookbook). She is a breast cancer survivor, and lives in an old Victorian with her husband, two children, and a sweet dog. You can often find her puttering in her garden. maryannemohanraj.com